My First Reiki Book

Caryn Block

Copyright

Published by Caryn M. Block
Copyright © 2016 Caryn M. Block
Cover Design by Caryn M. Block
Illustrations inspired by the artwork of Jan Settle

ISBN-978-1540463647
ISBN-1540463648
Library of Congress Catalog Number: 2016919615
Printed in the United States of America

Dedication

To the next generation. You are our greatest hope.

Acknowledgements

I couldn't have accomplished this task without the support of my family and friends. Special thanks to my wonderful friend, Jennifer Garver, who has mentored me all these years and to Mary Jo VanWingerden who advised me to take my first Reiki class.

Table of Contents

My First Reiki Book
By Caryn Block

Reiki is a special gift
 I can use when I am sore.
I put my hands upon myself
 and call the energy forth.

My hands feel all tingly warm
 with this special light.
Life force energy in our touch
 we clear away the blight.

Don't forget the chakras too
 need balancing and love.
Our bodies very own fixer-upper
an electric charge from above.

Take care of all your thoughts
And offer up gratitude
So when you're feeling really bad,
 you can improve your mood.

Place your hands upon your heart
and call in all God's peace.
Just say the phrase "Reiki On"
and let the energy release.

God's just waiting for your prayer
To make you feel all right.
Then move your hands to where it hurts
And experience the heavenly light.

Reiki is a special gift

I can use when I am sore.

I put my hands upon myself

and call the energy forth.

Reiki
On

My hands feel all tingly warm
with this special light.

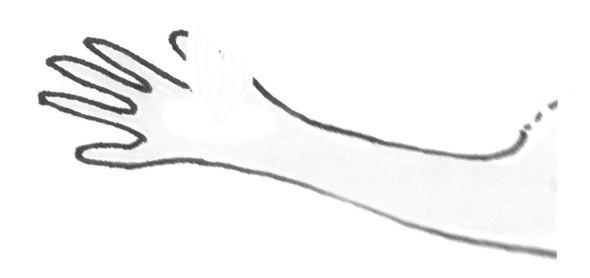

Life force energy in our touch
we clear away the blight.

Don't forget the chakras too need balancing and love.

Chakra System

Crown - Spiritual

3rd Eye - Perception

Throat - Communication

Heart - Love

Solar Plexus Power

Sacral - Self-Respect
/Expression

Root - Survival

Our bodies very own fixer-upper
an electric charge from above.

Take care of all your thoughts
And offer up gratitude,

So when you're feeling really bad,
you can improve your mood.

Place your hands upon your heart
and call in all God's peace.

Just say the phrase "Reiki On"
and let the energy release

Reiki On...

God's just waiting for your prayer
To make you feel all right.

Then move your hands to where it hurts
And experience the heavenly light.

Coloring Pages:

What does Reiki look like to you?

What do your Angels look like?

What are you grateful for?

1.

2.

3.

4.

5.

6.

7.

8.

9.

10.

Reiki Ideals

Just for today:

No Anger.

No Worries.

I will work to the best of my ability.

I will be kind to others.

I will be grateful for my many blessings.

For the Parents:

What is Reiki?

Reiki is a Japanese energy technique which uses the life force energy of the divine for stress reduction and relaxation, and to promote healing in the energy system of the human body. It is administered by the laying on of hands and anyone of any age can learn it.

The Japanese word Reiki is derived of two words; *Rei* and *Ki*. In this case, they translate roughly to *divine intelligence or God* for "Rei", and *energy or spirit* for "Ki."

Reiki treats the whole person, including body, mind, spirit and emotions, and usually feels like a warm glow that relaxes and sustains you. Many people have reported profound experiences.

Reiki does not depend on intellectual capacity or spiritual development so this technique is available to anyone including the very young.

When using this method with your child, remind them to breathe and connect to the divine. Have them call "Reiki On" either out loud or in their minds, and lay their hands over the area that is hurt or ill. They can stay in that position as long as it is comfortable for them.

While Reiki is spiritual in nature it is not a religion, nor is it a substitute for medical treatment. If your child is hurt or ill and needs medical care, please contact your doctor or emergency services immediately.

Education for the Children of 2012 and Beyond

I think that our educational structure needs to change drastically and, until it does, home schooling will be necessary. The children of the future will be more focused on creativity and hands-on learning. Memorization and drilling will not work for these sensitive souls. They will be born remembering that they have lived before. Authority figures will have to earn their respect, if they get it at all. For these children will know, without a shadow of a doubt, that they are just as capable and important in their learning as everyone else. No longer will they accept a teacher lording over them, making them feel inferior. They will know that they have experienced many lifetimes and have come to Earth to change it.

So how do we adults deal with this new paradigm? By bringing play back to learning. At an early age children need to be encouraged to play and imagine. To experience everything and experiment: physically, mentally, and spiritually. They should be encouraged to go inside and check in with their heart, or intuition, when something is causing discomfort or doesn't "feel right." Or go outside to connect with nature and the rhythms of life.

Self-love, as well as unconditional love, will need to be experienced and promoted. Teachers will need to become guides and mentors, making learning fun and giving each child a chance to enjoy the experience.

If a child shows an aptitude toward a certain field, they should be encouraged to follow it to the furthest conclusion. Education will need to be more specialized as these children figure out what they want to do. Everyone should be doing the work that they love. Only by thoroughly enjoying their work, will these children be happy and give something back to society.

About the Author

Caryn Block
I write about the paranormal, because my life is paranormal.

I saw my first ghost at three years of age and have been having paranormal experiences all of my life. This actually drove me to learn about God, and my gifts, to better understand them and learn to use them to help the world.

My mother was also sensitive and allowed me the freedom to discover what information was available at that time. I have since become a Reiki Master and Theta practitioner. I've owned a metaphysical store and learned about the tools available to help those of us willing to embrace our gifts to use them to our best advantage.

I also have had experiences where I wanted to "cry and run." I hope this book will help your child know they are not alone, nor do they need to be afraid. These gifts were given to us to learn about and use. They are not a curse, or evil, or witchcraft. They are gifts from God.

I began my writing career as a Paranormal Romance author. I love stories that end in "Happily Ever After." The paranormal part is because my life is paranormal. You can find these books under the pen name: Caryn Moya Block. These books are for adults and contain sexual relations between the hero and heroine. No peeking kids!

Now that I have become a grandparent, I want to help my granddaughters, and children in general, learn about their gifts. That desire is where the "Psychic Kids Series" manifested.

For more information about the "Psychic Kids Series," visit my website CarynBlock.com or you can write me at **carynblockpsychickids@gmail.com** .

Also by Caryn Block/ Caryn Moya Block

Enlighten Up Series
Joy, My Journey of Awakening

The Psychic Kid's Series
Feelings Not My Own

I See Spirits

My First Reiki Book

Illustrations Inspired by the Artwork of:

JAN SETTLE

*Color is the force that drives my artwork. It inspires me, motivates me
& affects every aspect of my life.*

My work in water media is an expression of my great love of life in general and for landscapes and animals in particular. As a child growing up in Culpeper, VA, I frequented art shows and art group meetings with my mother, a local artist. This started me on a life-long pursuit of colorful expression and design. These passions led me to Virginia Commonwealth University and a degree in Interior Design.

All these years later I am still using color to create beautiful living spaces and to express my perspective on the surrounding landscape and creatures. I began painting in a self-taught manner, but soon realized there was much to learn through associations with other artists. I am a member of the Windmore Foundation for the Arts, the Blue Ridge Art League and the Pastel Society of Virginia.

I currently live with my husband, our Australian Shepherd & 3 wonderful rescue cats, in Castleton, VA, at the foot of the beautiful Blue Ridge Mountains.
564 Aaron Mountain Road
Castleton, VA 22716
540.937.2294 Home   540.219.6259 Cell

CastleRockDesignsVA@yahoo.com
www.castlerockdesigns-va.com

Resources

These are sites I use and are in my opinion trustworthy. I am not an affiliate, nor do I receive any kind of compensation for listing them here. Any information you receive should be looked at with common sense. If it doesn't look or sound right then ignore it and move on. You will find the internet full of information. Some of it worthwhile and some of it not. Use caution.

http://www.reiki.org

http://www.angeltherapy.com

http://www.communicatewithangels.com

http://www.tut.com

http://www.thetahealing.com

http://www.louisehay.com/

http://www.angelsabound4u.com

CPSIA information can be obtained
at www.ICGtesting.com
Printed in the USA
LVHW071544121020
668589LV00002B/47